I0621321

RELATIVE TRUTH

a novella

DAN GRIFFIN

Copyright © 2018 *Relative Truth* by Dan Griffin

Published by Piscataqua Press
an imprint of RiverRun Bookstore
32 Daniel Street
Portsmouth NH 03801

ISBN: 978-1-944393-96-0

NOTICE TO THE READER

Thank you to Jeff Valluzzi, Matt Dadmun, Daphne Galatas, Agam Neiman, Jerri-lee Maille, John Maguire, Kellsey Metzger, and Dr. Edward Drummond for taking the time to read my manuscript and offer your insights. And of course, thank you to my trinity Ellen, Olivia, and Henry Griffin.

For Ellen on our 28th anniversary

CHAPTER ONE
The Ride to Boscawen, May 25, 2017

Eighteen years ago, Eva Guardia killed her six-year-old son.

Attorney Benjamin Truitt squeezed the clutch of his Sportster. *Eva killed her six-year-old boy. But it wasn't murder because murder requires criminal intent*, Ben thought. Ben tapped the shifter, heard the bike plunk into third gear, and eased out the clutch.

Warm air blew over his face as he rolled over the top of a hill on Route 27 in Candia, New Hampshire. The engine rumbled beneath him, and the road fell away, winding into Hooksett. The hills of Jaffrey and Dublin appeared in the distance, and beyond them Mount Monadnock faded against the horizon.

Ben had spent the morning studying the old police reports and psychiatric records from Eva's criminal case. *The reports said that three Manchester Police officers spotted Eva on the outside of the suicide fence of the Queen City bridge. The officers approached and tried to engage her. She kept her back to the officers and looked at them over her shoulder. She said nothing. One officer observed that she stared at them as if she was looking right through them.*

Ben rolled off the throttle. The engine quieted. He pulled in the clutch and coasted down the hill. His ears filled with a rush of wind.

The police spoke with Eva for some time. After a while, she dropped from the bridge into the river. This was 11:30 in the morning on November 2, 1999.

El Dia de Muertos, Truitt thought, *the Day of the Dead.*

She was saved by Manchester Fire and Rescue, fished out of the Merrimack River with a wound in her stomach.

The psychiatrists all later agreed that she was delusional, responding to internal stimuli, suffering auditory and visual hallucinations.

Ben wondered what Eva had experienced. He knew whatever it was, it was different from what the police and first responders saw and heard. He once had a schizophrenic client tell him that the world was very different on and off her medications.

"And you know," she had said, "it is a much more exciting world off my medications."

Ben wound along Route 3A, past the barn-red backside of the New Hampshire State Liquor Store, which advertised a special on Patron tequila.

CHAPTER TWO

A Perpetual Altar

Eva opened her front door the width of the chain lock and peeked out.

Ben extended his hand through the opening. "Hi, Eva," he said.

"Yes?" Eva's eyes moved from Ben's face to his hand.

"I'm Attorney Benjamin Truitt." Ben's hand hung in the air.

"Oh, yes, yes, come in." Eva unlatched the chain and opened the door just enough for Ben to squeeze through. Her small apartment was swept and decorated colorfully with Mexican folk art pieces. Brightly painted cats, turtles, and sea horses hung on the walls and perched on shelves. Some clothes were scattered here and there on the floor. A stale odor hung in the air, like the windows in the apartment had not been opened in years. An aquarium with murky water rested on an iron stand in one corner of the living area.

Ben sat on a couch and Eva sat on an overstuffed chair across from him. He pulled her file from his nylon computer bag and laid it on the table between them.

"It's a beautiful day," he said. *The police reports said that Eva was treated at the Elliot Hospital for a stab wound to the abdomen the day her son died.*

Eva glanced out the window. "Yes, I see," she said. "I haven't been out today."

"You should go out later. It must be seventy degrees, not humid at all." The dead apartment air stifled Ben. "Or at least open a window."

Eva shrugged. *According to the reports, Eva told a hospital staff worker that she had stabbed herself.*

"It's such a beautiful day," Ben said.

"OK." Eva stood and walked across the room. She moved as if her mind and body were not quite in-sync. She opened a window and let in a stream of sweet air.

Eva told the emergency room nurse that she sacrificed her six-year-old son, Emmanuel "Manny" Guardia. Eva said that Manny had been reading from the black bible, that Eva was like Jesus, that she was having bad dreams, that she was hearing voices, that her son was born evil, that this had all been prophesied. But now, she said, he could know peace.

Eva returned to the overstuffed chair and sunk into the cushions.

Ben noticed a small altar in the corner of the room by the window. The altar displayed carefully arranged marigolds and sugar skulls around its edges. A Santa Muerte figurine and a gold-framed photograph of a boy sat in the center.

The ER nurse took Eva's street address and gave it to the Manchester Police. The police broke down the door to Eva's apartment and found a dead little boy on the floor, his throat slashed, and his right eye plucked out. A twelve-inch knife with a carved bone handle rested across his chest.

"As I mentioned on the telephone," Ben said, flipping through the documents in his file, "the probate court appointed me to represent you in the involuntary admission hearing scheduled for next Thursday at the state hospital."

"Involuntary admission?" Eva poked her head out of the cushions. "I'm doing fine. I'm taking my meds. I'm working at the grocery store." Her hair was rust red but black at the roots. "I even got my driver's license." She leaned a little closer to Ben. "I thought they just wanted to extend my conditional discharge."

"They do," Ben said. "Don't worry. Nobody wants to send you back to the hospital again."

By court order, Eva had been held involuntarily at the state hospital for several years before she was released back to the community. As long as she took her medications, attended her therapy sessions, and refrained from dangerous behaviors, she was relatively free to live her life. If she didn't follow these conditions, she could be re-admitted to the psychiatric hospital until the doctors deemed her safe to return home.

Ben saw movement in the aquarium across the room. A black and orange turtle popped its head above the surface of the water and then sounded for the bottom, churning green algae in its wake.

Eva dropped her shoulders to her side and rested back into the chair.

Ben watched a cloud of sadness move over Eva's face, then something else, something different flashed across her face, as she sunk deeper into the cushion and folded her arms across her chest.

The ER nurse described Eva as having a hate stare.

"Yes," Ben said, "yes. Everybody seems to agree that you are doing well."

After Manny's body was found and after Eva was released from the hospital, she was taken to the Secure Psychiatric Unit (SPU) at the New Hampshire State Prison in Concord. The SPU staff observed her to be in distress. She answered questions with considerable delay and seemed suspicious of her surroundings. She appeared depressed and delusional. "Gas in a room," she said. "I would want to be with my kids if I died." She was fearful. She was thought blocking. "My son was evil. He read from the black bible. My brother saw, too." Eva was diagnosed with schizoaffective disorder.

"So," Ben continued, "they are looking to extend your conditional discharge for five years."

"Five years?" Eva leaned forward and rested her forearms on her thighs.

"Yes, that is the most the court can order at any one time."

"But the court could order less?"

"Yes, but given the history of your case..."

"That's OK," Eva said. "I'm fine with it. Five years is fine."

"I could ask the assistant attorney general and the psychiatrists if they would agree to less."

"No, no," Eva said, "it's OK."

"OK, then," Ben said and stood up. He looked at the altar across the room. "Is that an ofrenda?"

"Yes. You know ofrenda?"

"Si, claro," Ben said.

"Bien."

"…and Santa Muerte." Ben pointed to the holy death figurine, the protector of outlaws, outcasts, and outliers.

"Santa Muerte," Eva said. "Yes."

"And the little boy in the photo, is that…"

"Manny."

The little turtle swam along the side of the aquarium and scratched the glass with its claws. Eva picked up some scattered clothes from the floor and walked Ben to the door and showed him out.

CHAPTER THREE

The Price of Clarity

Ben decided to take the long way home. The car was all about the fastest way. The bike was all about the most scenic and head-clearing way home. He took Route 27 through the hills of Hooksett and Candia. He pulled in the clutch and leaned into the right by the Candia Congregational Church and slid down South Road. He wound into Auburn, glided by the lakeshore, and climbed and coasted down the hills. He rolled southbound down Chester Road. The wind and the engine rumble filled his ears. A chipmunk popped out of a hole on the side of the road and shot onto the pavement. Ben pulled in his clutch and touched his brakes. The chipmunk ratcheted its tail and spun circles in the road before darting off, disappearing into the shadow of the woods.

Ben released the clutch and brakes and cranked the throttle. He rolled up behind a guy and girl on a bagger. Bits of music from the bagger's radio caught Ben's ears.

The guy wore an American flag helmet and shooter's glasses. The girl wore a flat black bobber helmet and goggles. Her ponytail snapped in the breeze behind her.

Ben wanted to free his mind from Eva's story, but it was going to take more miles. The bagger slowed and leaned into a tight corner, then accelerated through the turn. *Good*, Ben thought, and decided to try to keep a steady interval between the two bikes as best he could. He slowed into the curve and accelerated, matching the bagger's speed about twenty feet behind.

When psychotic people experience hallucinations and delusions, the hallucinations and delusions are real to them, as real to them as the blue bagger with the POW/MIA flag was real to Ben right now. Ben knew that. That lesson was reinforced time and again over his years of practice. The dream is reality to the dreamer.

But now, Ben thought, *for years, Eva's been medicated. She's lucid. She carries what she did.*

Ms. Guardia was diagnosed as psychotic and began taking antipsychotic and antidepressant medication, the reports said. At SPU, she asked another patient to help her kill herself. The patient told staff. The SPU staff asked her about it, and she said she was "probably having a bad day."

The bagger started up a hill that wound slowly to the right past a grey Cape, which was set off the road behind pines and birches. Ben started his climb still twenty feet behind the bagger. He cracked the throttle and felt the torque tug him up the hill and heard the throaty engine sound.

Eva underwent several psychiatric evaluations for the purpose of determining her competency to stand trial for murder. All the psychiatrists agreed. Eva suffered from paranoid psychotic symptoms. She suffered auditory hallucinations, delusional thinking, bizarre ideation. She exhibited abnormal staring. She was detached from reality and could not meaningfully assist in her own defense. The judge found her not competent to stand trial.

A loaded log truck bombed northbound on Chester Road. Ben watched the bagger buckle and the blonde's ponytail whip in the wind as the log truck blew past them. Ben braced himself.

Back at SPU, Eva progressed for a while, then refused medications and relapsed. The SPU psychiatrist noted that she continued to develop delusional ideas about what was happening around her, delusional preoccupations similar to those of the Day of the Dead 1999, delusions that included a widespread conspiracy to frame her for the murder of her son.

A blast of wind from the logging truck hit Ben in the face and chest and wobbled his bike.

One psychiatrist opined that Eva had a "delusional system" that accompanied her psychosis, which had "paranoid themes." She believed that there was a plot against her that resulted in Emmanuel's death and her incarceration at SPU. She accused her half-brother in El Paso Texas of masterminding the plot.

Ben slowed to a stop at the blinking red light at the intersection of Route 102 and Chester Road. The bagger idled ahead of him. Ben signaled a left turn toward Raymond and Epping. The bagger rolled straight through the intersection toward Sandown. Ben leaned left onto Route 102 and Flag Helmet and Ponytail gave him the low biker wave as he turned. He nodded back, hands full of clutch and throttle.

He took the longer way home through Freemont to Epping. He needed a little more time to clear Eva's story from his mind. But these dark things sink into the psyche.

"Sometimes, I don't know how you do the work you do," he could hear his wife, Beth, say. "Seriously, these things take their toll on you."

Ben pictured Beth in her garden, then imagined Eva swallowed by the cushions in her chair. After a while, the wind and the road took his mind to other things.

CHAPTER FOUR

Eva's Hearing, Thursday, June 1, 2017

Ben wiped his feet on the rug in the vestibule entrance to New Hampshire Hospital and waited for the automatic doors to part. He stepped into the lobby, and the old guard motioned him around the metal detector.

"How are you doing today, Attorney Truitt?" the old man asked.

"Well, I'm working," Ben said.

The guard straightened on his stool and pulled on the lapels of his blue blazer. "If only we had been born rich instead of beautiful," he said.

"It is the curse of our lives," Ben said over his shoulder. He waved to the two receptionists behind the glass, who smiled and waved back. The guard pressed a buzzer and Ben heard the interior door click. He pulled the door open and walked to the elevator.

The Sixth Circuit Probate Court kept a tiny courtroom on the second floor of the New Hampshire Hospital. The courtroom measured about twelve by fifteen feet. The judge's bench and the witness stand occupied the front third of the courtroom. The lawyer's tables took up the middle of the room and a row of plastic chairs for witnesses lined the wall in the back. The court reporter sat with his tape recorder at a little desk against the wall to the left of the lawyer's tables, and the court officer pressed himself against the same wall. Every Thursday, the court sat to hear anywhere from five to eleven involuntary admissions cases. When court was in session, the court officer locked the doors and only the parties, lawyers, court personnel, and witnesses to a case were allowed into the proceeding. Ben had two cases on today's docket, Eva Guardia and Pamela Magoro.

A large skylight lit the waiting area outside of the courtroom. Lawyers and clients talked in corners. Witnesses sat on the blue couches along the walls. Hospital staff pushed carts of food and walked therapy dogs along the hallways.

The hospital paralegal shuffled up to Ben with his clipboard. "We're going to take Ms. Magoro's case first," he said.

"Oh, OK," Ben said.

"Yeah." The paralegal peered over his half-frame glasses. "We have a couple of witnesses on that case from the mental health center who are only going to be available for an hour or so this morning, so we wanted to get that one right in."

Ben took a seat on one of the couches, pulled his cellphone from his pocket, and scrolled through his email. He reviewed the facts and legal arguments for Ms. Magoro's case in his mind.

A few minutes later, Pamela Magoro lumbered down the hallway toward the courtroom with a hospital worker at each arm. She stood taller than both workers and the three formed something of a pyramid shape tottering down the hall. She grinned at Ben when she saw him.

"Are you ready?" Ben stood from the couch and walked with Ms. Magoro to the courtroom. The two hospital workers fell in behind them.

"I ready," she said. "I told you. I no mental." Ms. Magoro's eyes were always open wide, exposing the roundness of her eyeballs and giving her a perpetual look of surprise.

"I know you did," Ben said. According to the records in her hospital file, Ms. Magoro was born in Chad and came to America twenty years ago when she was seventeen.

"And I not hurt nobody," she said.

"That's right," Ben said. "Let's give them hell."

Ms. Magoro smiled her big smile and wiped the corners of her eyes with a tissue.

Ben couldn't help but like Pamela Magoro. She stood tall and strong with a resonant voice, and she carried herself upright with dignity.

On direct examination, Ms. Magoro's therapist testified that during one session Ms. Magoro hollered at the therapist and accused her of being from the "bad tribe." The therapist said that Ms. Magoro got up from her chair and "moved aggressively" toward her. The therapist said she was scared and asked Ms. Magoro to leave several times before Ms. Magoro finally left.

"She lying," Ms. Magoro shouted.

The judge shot a glance at Ben.

"Sorry, judge." Ben leaned over to Ms. Magoro's. "You'll get your chance to speak," he whispered.

"Was there anything else about Ms. Magoro that caused you concern?" the hospital lawyer asked.

"She expressed delusional beliefs."

"Like what?"

"Well," the therapist leaned forward toward the witness microphone, and pushed her blond hair behind her ears, "she believes that Osama Bin Ladin is holding her children hostage. She believes that she has children with John F. Kennedy, Mohammad Ali, and Nelson Mandela."

Pamela Magoro stopped dabbing the corners of her eyes and went rigid in her chair.

When the hospital rested its case, Ms. Magoro insisted on testifying on her own behalf. She testified that she was "not mental," that she didn't need medication, and that she never threatened or harmed Ms. Jones or anyone else.

On cross-examination, the hospital lawyer asked Ms. Magoro if she thought her therapist was from the bad tribe.

"What?" Ms. Magoro laughed. "She's white. She's not from no tribe."

The judge grinned.

"Do you believe that Osama Bin Laden is holding your children hostage?" the hospital lawyer asked.

"What? Osama Bin Laden. That's crazy. Osama Bin Laden is dead."

Ben straightened a little in his chair.

"Do you believe that you have children with Mohammad Ali?"

"No." Ms. Magoro twisted the tissue in her hands.

"Do you believe that you have children with John F. Kennedy?"

"JFK," Ms. Magoro snorted. "No, no way."

Ben and the judge smiled.

"Do you believe you have children with Nelson Mandela?"

Ms. Magoro leaned back in the witness chair and grinned. "Yes," she said, "Nelson and I have children."

"And where are these children now?" the hospital lawyer asked.

"They're safe," Ms. Magoro said, still beaming. "They're taken care of."

The hospital lawyer sat, and Ben popped to his feet.

"Is there anything about having children with Nelson Mandela that makes you want to hurt yourself?" Ben asked.

"What, no, why would it?"

"Is there anything about having children with Nelson Mandela that makes you want to hurt other people?"

"No."

Ms. Magoro stepped down from the witness box and extended her hand to Ben. "Thank you," she said.

"My pleasure."

"What happens now?"

"Well," Ben said, "the judge is going to think about the case and make a decision. We should know in a couple of days."

"What do you think?" Ms. Magoro asked, eyes wide and watery.

"I think you did all right." Ben didn't have the heart to tell her she had lost. She clearly suffered from a mental illness, and her aggressive episode with her therapist showed that she was potentially dangerous.

The two hospital workers escorted Ms. Magoro down the hallway and back to the locked unit.

Eva Guardia was sitting on a bench in the hallway by the courtroom when Ben stepped out. He sat next to her and pulled her file from his briefcase.

The hospital paralegal hurried over to them with his clipboard. "We've got a guy coming over from SPU." He looked up at Ben and Eva and pushed his glasses back up his nose. "We'll take that one next," he said, "and we'll do Ms. Guardia's case after that."

"Sounds good. Thank you."

The paralegal stepped away. Ben watched him move from lawyer to lawyer, advising them how many cases were before theirs and about when they could expect to be called into court.

"It shouldn't be too long," Ben said to Eva.

"OK," she said.

"Any questions?" Ben asked.

"No, not really."

"All right," Ben said, flipping through Eva's file.

Eva stared at her feet.

Ben looked through Eva's social history again. *She was born in El Paso Texas to Mexican American parents. Her mother died when she was four. Her father remarried a year later, a Caucasian woman with some possible Apache ancestry. Her father's second wife may have had substance abuse and mental health problems and was frequently gone from the home. After a few years, she left and never returned. Her father was reportedly an alcoholic and may have beaten the children. Social services responded to several reports of concern over the years but never removed the children from the home. Eva and her little brother developed a close bond and were described as inseparable. In high school, both Eva and her brother were showing signs of mental illness.*

"Can they-?" Eva said quietly. "Is there a chance they could make me go to trial on the criminal charges?"

"Is it possible?" Ben answered, "yes. Is it likely? No."

Eva nodded her head.

"I think the prosecutors understand what happened. I think everyone understands that you--" Ben searched for his next words, "that you were very sick, that you didn't understand…"

"Yes," Eva said and looked at the floor, ending the conversation.

When Eva was about twenty-three, she traveled to England for several months. What she did there is unknown. After England, she showed up in New Hampshire, pregnant. She never disclosed the identity of the father.

The hospital elevator doors pulled open and a man in an orange jumpsuit and shackles rattled out with a deputy sheriff on either side of him. The man was thin and muscular with a shaved head. Half of his face was covered in a tribal tattoo. He had wild green eyes.

"Attorney Truitt," the man said as he passed by Ben. "Eva," the man said and nodded, as he passed Eva.

"Jakob," Eva said.

"Take good care of my sister, Attorney Truitt," the prisoner called over his shoulder, "like you took good care of Gina."

"All right, that's enough," one of the deputies said, as he tightened his grip on the prisoner's elbow and pushed him through the courtroom door.

The bald head and face tattoo threw Ben for a bit but then he remembered. "Jakob Snyder is your brother?"

Eva nodded yes. "Half-brother," she said.

Jakob Snyder emerged from the closed courtroom half an hour later. The deputies double-timed him to the elevator, and he was gone in a flash. He shot Ben a grin just before the elevator doors closed.

"When was the last time you saw him?" Ben asked.

Eva didn't answer. She just shook her head.

Eva's hearing lasted about three minutes. The parties identified themselves for the record, advised the judge that there was an agreement to continue Eva's conditional discharge for an additional five years. The judge said, "Very well," turned to Eva and said, "I wish you the best, Ms. Guardia."

CHAPTER FIVE

Winter Discontent, February 17, 2009

Eight years before Ben met Eva Guardia, he agreed to meet Billie Napolitano and her cousin, Gina Cataldo, at MaryAnn's Diner on East Broadway in Derry. When Ben stepped out of the cold and into the diner, he spotted Billie and cousin Gina sitting in a chrome and black vinyl upholstered booth by a window overlooking Broadway. Side-by-side portraits of Audrey Hepburn and Marilyn Monroe hung on the wall to the right of the window.

Ben took a seat across from the two women.

"Why didn't you return my first telephone call?" Billie asked.

Ben looked up from his menu. "To be honest, I forgot you called."

"Oh." Billie's eyes narrowed a bit, and she looked out the window at the falling rain and snow.

Ben watched Billie. "A wintry mix," he offered.

"Mmmmm," Billie replied.

The smells of bacon, coffee, and maple syrup filled the diner. Roy Orbison played on the jukebox.

"Look," Ben said, "sometimes I forget things."

Billie turned her gaze to Ben and then back out the window. "That's new," she said.

"No, really," he said. "I have Lyme Disease." Ben turned his mug upwards. A waitress in a black poodle skirt and a red top stopped by the booth.

"Do you all need a minute?" the waitress asked and filled the three cups with coffee.

"Yes, please," Billie said. The waitress disappeared along the black and white checkered floor into the crowded diner.

"I've been sick for about three years, now." Ben said. "I have four or five lucid hours a day then I'm semi-conscious on the couch for about nineteen hours, praying to die. I get up the next morning exhausted and depressed and do it again."

Billie looked out the window then back at Ben. She tore open a packet of sweetener and poured it into her mug. "I'm sorry," she said. "I had no idea."

"Sounds horrible," Gina said, her voice soft and congested.

Ben poured cream into his coffee and watched the two women across from him do the same. "Too much information, right," he said and stirred the cream with a teaspoon.

"Yeah," Billie said.

"No," Gina said, "it's all right."

"Anyway," Ben said, "what can I do for you guys?"

Billie and Gina studied their menus.

The waitress circled back to the booth and topped off the three coffees. "Are you all ready to order or do you need more time?" she asked.

Ben ordered the Portuguese omelet with linguica sausage and feta cheese. Gina ordered a small garden salad with balsamic vinaigrette dressing, and Billie ordered a mushroom and swiss burger.

"Will you help my cousin?" Billie asked, when the waitress was out of sight.

Billie and Ben had attended the night program at Suffolk Law School together. They endured four years of working all day, sitting in classes all night, and studying all weekend. Billie even took a day off work to watch Ben try his first case as a student at the Somerville District Court. Ben got a not guilty verdict defending a hit-and-run case. After that, Billie would always greet Ben with, "my favorite lawyer."

"What's going on?" Ben asked.

Gina looked down at the metal-flake Formica table top.

Billie sat quietly.

Gina was fairer than Billie, but they shared the same gentle features. Gina's face was scrubbed clean of make-up, and she avoided Ben's eyes. Gina reminded Ben of a delicate lamp with a dimmer switch. At the moment, her light was turned low.

"Look," Ben said, "no judgment here."

Gina adjusted the napkin in her lap.

"It's OK," Billie said.

The waitress returned to the booth and delivered the plates and a bottle of ketchup.

After she left, Gina told her story. She was twenty-seven. She married John Cataldo when she was nineteen. Mr. Cataldo was sixty-three. They had two children in their first two years of marriage. Mr. Cataldo was her first and only lover when they married. Mr. Cataldo was "a kind man," Gina said, and Billie nodded. Three years ago, Mr. Cataldo died.

"I'm sorry," Ben said.

Mr. Cataldo left Gina with four children, a big colonial house, and seven acres of wooded land three miles down a logging road in New Canaan.

About two weeks after Mr. Cataldo's passing, a man came to Gina's door. She had seen him around town. He was blond, thin, muscular, handsome, mid-thirties. He was exciting, a bit wild. He had blazing green eyes.

"So far, so good," Ben joked.

Gina brightened a little.

"He just showed up at your front door?"

"Yes."

"What's his name?"

"Jakob Snyder," she said.

Billie eyed Ben. "Sound familiar?"

"Yes, a little," Ben said. "But I'm not sure why."

"Jakob Snyder," Gina continued, "but he calls himself Gotal."

"Gotal?" Ben asked.

"It's Apache. It means Coyote."

"Wait, Jakob Snyder is Apache?"

Gina shrugged. "Well..."

"Blond hair, green eyes..."

"...he believes he is." Gina paused. Her brow furrowed. "He may actually have some Apache blood. I don't know."

"OK," Ben said, "sorry."

"He believes he is a great spirit man, like Geronimo."

"OK."

"He is charismatic," Gina continued.

"Svengali," Billie said. "Like a Jim Jones kind of character."

Jakob "Gotal" Snyder moved in. He was good with the kids. He taught them Apache words, chanted them to sleep. He spent hours in the woods. He built bonfires and danced around them with Gina and the kids. He was full of life. He grew weed and smoked it in ceremonial pipes. He had prophetic visions and told the future. Things he saw came to pass.

"Really?"

"I know," Gina said. "It sounds crazy now, but it seemed real at the time."

Jakob wanted to raise horses on Gina's land, live the old ways. Gina kicked him out for a while after he maxed out her credit card on internet porn and tried to put her house up for collateral for a horse farm.

He was back at her front door two weeks later, hat in hand. He had nowhere else to go. No one else to go to. He moved back in again; his wild-eyed charisma filled the house. Jakob built Gina a moon lodge, a sacred place for women.

"Moon lodge? Is that a real Apache thing?" Ben asked.

"Yes," Gina said. "Well, maybe more of a plains Indian thing from what I can tell, but it all seemed to be something of a jumble in Jakob's head anyway."

Gina gave birth to two children in the moon lodge, Cocheta, a girl, and Gurbachan, a boy. Cocheta means "unknown" and Gurbachan means "promise of the spirit man."

At some point, Jacob's ex-wife Janine and his thirteen-year-old daughter, Chase, moved into the big colonial in the woods in New Canaan. Janine's boyfriend also moved in for a while until he and Jakob fought, and the boyfriend fled.

"Oh, no." Ben remembered the Union Leader article from a few days ago. "New Canaan man arrested on incest charges," he said.

Gina's features darkened. She pulled a newspaper clipping from her purse and handed it to Ben.

"Jakob Snyder was arrested last Wednesday for incest with a teenage girl," Ben read aloud. "Chase?" he asked.

"Yes," Gina said.

Billie nodded.

"At your house?"

Gina nodded.

"Let me guess," Ben said. "They charged you with 'Endangering the Welfare of a Child?'"

"Yes."

Ben and Billie locked eyes. Gina stared into her swirling coffee.

"OK, I'll do it," Ben said.

"Thanks, Ben," Billie said. "We have a thousand dollars we can give you now as a retainer."

"That's all right," Ben said. "Keep it. Let me do some work, and I will bill you as I go."

Ben turned to Gina. "Pay me as you can. A single mother with all those kids…"

Gina nodded still staring into her coffee mug.

"Is there something more?" Ben asked. "Like I said, no moral judgments here."

"There's another charge." Gina brought the mug to her lips.

"What's that?" Ben asked.

Gina sipped her coffee. "Sexual assault, statutory rape," she whispered.

"Oh." Ben sat back down. "Well," he said, "the Goffstown Court has jurisdiction over New Canaan, so I know you have a good judge and a fair-minded prosecutor."

The waitress dropped the check at their table. Billie grabbed it and pointed out the window. The rain and snow mixture had turned into fluffy flakes and snow was piling up rapidly on the sidewalks and streets.

"Looks like we are not going anywhere for a while," Billie said. "Maybe we should get some pie."

The three stayed at the diner for another hour or two, eating blueberry pie and drinking coffee, while the plows and sanders worked the streets. Billie and Ben swapped stories from law school, and all three talked about their hopes for the future. Billie planned to retire from the law soon and buy a boat and fish the Maine coast. Ben wanted to not be sick anymore, and Gina longed to get all the Jakob Snyder nastiness behind her.

CHAPTER SIX

Probable Cause, Tuesday, February 24, 2009

The Goffstown Court sat in the basement of the town hall, down two flights of stairs, through a narrow corridor and past a couple of closeted rooms, where a lawyer and client could speak in confidence, if they spoke softly.

Ben and Gina sat side by side on one of the oak benches behind the bar, shoulder to shoulder with other lawyers and defendants. Fluorescent lights buzzed overhead. Gina fidgeted with a tube of cherry chapstick, and Ben studied the annotations in his criminal statutes book.

Tony Shevchenko stepped up behind Ben. "Ben, I told you," he said, "don't read those books. We'll tell you what the law is when you get here."

Ben looked over his shoulder and smiled.

Shev stood about six-four. He was a lawyer, the New Canaan prosecutor, and a captain in the New Canaan Police Department. He wore brown and white wingtip shoes and a gun under his suit coat.

A few days ago, Shev handed Ben all the state's discovery on Gina's case: police reports, interview transcripts, video-recordings of interviews, and photographs.

Ben went through it all. *Fourteen-year-old Chase and mother Janine flew to El Paso, Texas, after Chase got pregnant with Jakob Snyder's baby. Gina helped them with money for the flight and for an abortion at an El Paso clinic.*

Ben put his index finger in the statute book to hold his place and closed it. "Tony," he said, "this is Ms. Catalado."

"Nice to meet you," Shev said.

"Nice to meet you, too." Gina whispered.

In El Paso, Chase started seeing a boy. She told the boy what happened in New Hampshire. The boy encouraged her to tell the El Paso police. The El Paso police notified the New Canaan police, and Officers Troy and Newton flew to El Paso to interview Chase and Janine.

Chase told the police that she and Snyder had sex at Gina's house in New Canaan. Chase said it happened many times over many months. She said that Snyder wanted Chase and Gina to have sex while he watched. "Mostly," Chase said, "we just rubbed each other's backs and shoulders. One time, I think, I might have touched Gina's boob."

Ben rested the book on his thigh. "Hey," he said, "when you get a minute can we talk about resolving Ms. Cataldo's case?"

"Oh, I see how it is." Shev looked at Gina and grinned. "Here it comes, he's going to beat me down like a bargain basement sale."

Gina twiddled the chapstick tube in her hand and turned from Shev to Ben.

"It's the second charge," Ben said, "the sexual assault. I've read the police reports and interviews. I've been going over the statute, and..."

Shev threw his hands up. "See that's the problem," he said. "That's why I don't want you reading law." He laughed. "I'll be happy to talk with you later." He patted Ben on the shoulder, nodded to Gina and crossed the bar to the prosecutor's table.

Officer Newton arrested and interviewed Snyder when he got back to New Hampshire. Snyder admitted that he had sexual relations with Chase. "In many cultures," Snyder said, "it is the responsibility of the men to teach the girls, you know, the ways of being a woman." Officer Newton asked him if it was an Apache custom for fathers to sleep with their daughters. Snyder said it was not. Snyder explained that he was a spirit warrior, that he struggled on a spiritual plane against an evil that pervaded our minds and inhabited our law enforcement and courts. Snyder fought for integration and wholeness and love.

Ben and Gina were talking about the weather and family, when Snyder clanged into the courtroom, hands and feet shackled like Jacob Marley's ghost. He sat on the back bench with the sheriff. Gina averted her eyes and lowered her head. Her face dimmed in shadow.

Snyder was thin with long, dirty blond hair and green eyes. He looked windblown in his orange jumpsuit. His expression was feral. His eyes darted all over the courtroom from person to person to window to judge to floor. His thighs bounced like pistons in a revving motor.

Ben caught Snyder's eyes. Snyder stared back without blinking, smiled a little, then locked his gaze to the back of Gina's head.

Ben turned to Gina. Her body went rigid beside him, and she bowed her head lower. Ben made small talk to calm her. He told her about how much he loved to paint and cook and about how he always had dinner ready for his wife when she returned home from her long train ride from Cambridge. He talked about his son's music and his daughter's love of theater.

Gina raised her head a bit and applied some chapstick to her lips. She told Ben about her children's love of dance and drawing.

"The matter of the State of New Hampshire versus Gina Cataldo," the court officer called.

"We're up," Ben whispered to Gina. "This should be relatively quick and painless."

The two crossed the bar and took their seats at the defendant's table.

"Good morning, your honor," Ben said.

The judge studied the criminal complaints in his hands. "We're here for a probable cause hearing?"

"An arraignment," Shev said, standing. "I've reduced the charges to misdemeanors. So, we'll be keeping them here in district court."

"Ok," the judge said, "you and Attorney Truitt have had some discussions then?"

"Yes, judge," Shev said.

"And how does your client plead, Attorney Truitt?"

"Not guilty on both charges."

"Very well," the judge said and turned to the clerk. "We'll set a date for trial, then."

The clerk studied her calendar. "May fifth at 10 AM."

The judge handed Gina's paperwork to the clerk and reached for the next stack of criminal complaints. "I wish you well, Ms. Cataldo," he said.

Ben walked Gina out of the courtroom, staying between her and Snyder as they exited.

"A trial," Gina said as they stepped into the hallway. "I don't want a trial."

"I know," Ben said.

"I told you, I'm willing to plead guilty. I just want to get this all behind me and move on." Gina's voice broke a little.

"I know, I know," Ben said. "I'm looking out for you. Just let me work for you, please."

Gina sighed and nodded her head.

"Good," Ben said. "We'll talk soon."

"You're not leaving?"

"No, I think I'm going to stay and watch some of Jakob's hearing," Ben said.

"Oh."

Ben hesitated at the threshold to the courtroom. "Are you OK?" he asked. "Are you going to be all right? This must have been the first time that you saw him since..."

"I'll be all right," Gina said. "Really. Go back in."

When Ben entered the courtroom, he saw Snyder perched at the defendant's table in his dirty orange jumpsuit, a public defender beside him. Officer Gary Newton was testifying from the witness stand. Officer Newton's black hair, badge and gun all shined under the courtroom lights.

"At this time," Officer Newton said, "Officer Jones and I proceeded to Six Goodman Young Way, New Canaan, New Hampshire, in our four-wheel drive vehicle."

"Was there some reason why you took the four-wheeler?" Shev asked.

"Yes," Newton continued. "Six Goodman Young Way is located about three miles down an old logging road and it had been snowing and raining. Given the difficult terrain, Officer Troy and I decided to proceed in the New Canaan Police four-wheel drive vehicle for safety."

"I see," Shev said. He rubbed his thumb and index finger along his thick mustache to hide his grin. "What, if anything, happened when you got to the house?"

"Jakob Snyder met us in the front yard. I brought up the allegations that he had impregnated his daughter, who lived in Texas."

"What did Mr. Snyder say to that?" Shev asked.

"Initially he denied any knowledge of the allegations; however, eventually he stated that they were true, that…"

"They are true," Snyder blurted from the defense table. His public defender, red-faced, pulled him by the shoulder and whispered in his ear.

"Counsel," the judge said, "you might want to advise your client to keep quiet."

"Yes, your honor."

"Continue," the judge said turning back to Shev and Officer Newton.

"He said that it was all true, that he did have sexual relations with his daughter on numerous occasions and that he did eventually impregnate her."

Shev paused and let the words hang in the air before his next question. "After Mr. Snyder admitted to impregnating his own daughter, what did you and the other officer do?"

"At that point," Newton said, "we told Snyder that he was under arrest as he had admitted to a serious crime. We then ended the conversation. I handcuffed Mr. Snyder and proceeded to place him in the back of the four-wheel drive cruiser."

"Thank you, Officer Newton. I have no more questions at this time," Shev said and took his seat at the prosecutor's table.

The public defender popped up. "Officer Newton," he said, "you talked to Mr. Snyder about more than his daughter that night correct?"

"I'm not sure what you mean," Newton responded.

"He told you that he had been engaged in a battle on a spiritual plane, correct?"

Shev jumped to his feet. "Objection, your honor, relevance?"

The judge motioned Shev to sit back down. "I'll allow it," he said. "You may answer the question, Officer Newton."

"Yes, he said he was battling on a spiritual dimension."

"He said that he had been fighting this spiritual battle for one-hundred years, correct?"

Snyder straightened his spine against his chair.

Officer Newton glanced at Snyder. "Yes," he said.

"It's true. It's all true," Snyder blurted, "but you need to hear how they have been mistreating me in the jail..." Snyder tried to rise from his seat, but the public defender held him down with a hand on his shoulder.

"Mr. Snyder, please," the judge said, "you need to be quiet and let your lawyer speak for you."

Snyder stopped struggling.

The public defender turned back to Newton. "He also told you that a Native American lodge in the woods in New Canaan was a portal to another dimension, true?"

"Yes," Newton answered. "That's what he said."

"Did you give credence to any of his statements about portals to other dimensions and hundred-year spiritual battles?"

Officer Newton looked confused.

"Did you believe him when he told you about that stuff?"

"No," Newton answered.

"But you believed him when he said he was having sex with his daughter?"

"OK," Judge Herbert said, "I've heard enough. I'm finding probable cause." Judge Herbert turned his gaze to the defendant's table.

"Mr. Snyder…"

"Gotal," Snyder said.

"Mr. Snyder," the judge repeated. "I wish you well. Counsel," the judge said turning to the public defender, "I assume you will be raising competency at the superior court."

"Yes, your honor."

"Good. Next case."

Ben caught up to Shev in the parking lot behind the town hall. Shev was scraping ice off the windshield of his Ford pickup.

"Shev," Ben called.

"Oh, no," Shev said, turning around to see Ben. "I almost got away." He extended his hand and the two men shook. "Hey," he said and laughed, "I fight evil on spiritual and temporal planes every day."

"Sure, you do," Ben said. He could feel Lyme disease beginning to lock up his body and cloud his mind.

"That guy was a piece of work, right?" Shev looked Ben up and down. "Are you all right? You look like shit."

"Thanks," Ben said. "I'm all right. It's the Lyme disease. It only gives me a few hours a day before it pulls me under."

"I'm sorry, man," Shev said.

"The worst part is the depression." Ben rubbed his temples. "I'll tell you Shev, if I didn't have a family…"

"You've told me."

"Anyway, about Gina…"

"Here we go...Lyme disease hasn't stopped your lawyering," Shev said. "What about Gina?"

"She'll plead to the endangering charge and a no-time deal."

"No time?"

"She's got kids, and she's alone."

"And the sexual assault?"

"Shev, she's not a sex offender."

"Oh, she's not?"

"Look at the law and the girl's statement. Chase said that Snyder made Gina and Chase touch each other."

"Gina was naked in a bed with a teenage girl who touched her breast."

"But the statute says that the touching has got to be for the gratification of the offender. If anything, it was done for Snyder's gratification."

Shev opened the truck door and tossed his ice scrapper onto the bench seat and pulled himself into the cab. He rolled down the window. "You're right," he said. His breath fogged in front of his face. "I'll drop the sexual assault. She'll plead to the endangering charge, six months in the house of corrections, suspended for two years on good behavior."

"One year good behavior."

"Ben."

"Ok, two years good behavior, done."

Shev rolled up the window, put the truck in reverse, and backed away about six feet. He braked and rolled down the window. "Hey," he called to Ben.

"Yeah?"

"We haven't had a beer at the Ukrainian Club in a while."

"Well," Ben said, "first, that place is a pit…"

"And?"

"And I am English and Irish by descent…"

"And?"

"And I've been kind of busy with the Lyme disease and the suicidal ideations and planning and everything."

Ben watched Shev's truck slip into the night. Cold traveled up his body and stung his hands as fatigue and depression washed over him. His knees and elbows ached, and it was getting hard to move. He eased himself to his car and hoped he could make it home before his body failed and his mind faded.

CHAPTER SEVEN

The Love of a Fine Woman, Saturday, August 29, 2009

Ben slept until ten in the morning. He woke up a little less sick and tired than when he had gone to sleep twelve hours before. The depression still hung on him. Sometimes it weighed heavily, sometimes less so, but it was always there. He thought he had grown depressed because he had been sick for so many years, but his doctor told him that Lyme causes chemical changes in the brain that are consistent with depression. *Mental illness by bug*, he thought. His plan for the day was to paint and cook. He hoped his disease would give him until about four o'clock before it took him down again.

Ben grabbed a cup of coffee from the kitchen and walked down the hallway to his studio. He smelled linseed and clove oils. Warm morning air and sunlight filtered through the window screen.

He picked up a tube of titanium white and squeezed a large pile of paint onto one corner of his pallet. Then he squeezed out a large pile of ivory black on the opposite corner.

He saw Beth in the backyard loading handfuls of brush into a little green wheelbarrow. She wore blue jeans and gardening gloves.

"Bug spray?" Ben called through the screen.

"Yes, yes," Beth said, turning toward the window. "Good morning."

"Ticks, bugs," Ben called back, "they are going to rule the world."

"I know," Beth said grinning, "you've told me."

"You laugh, but in twenty years, all that will be left will be beautiful green earth—ticks, roaches and Keith Richards..."

"So, I've heard."

"... and twenty years from then, only Keith. "

Beth turned back to her yard work.

"I know these things," Ben shouted in mock indignity through the screen. "No prophet is honored in his own backyard."

"You've got that right," Beth shouted back.

Ben took a pallet knife and separated out about half of the pile of black paint into another pile and added a little white, making a dark gray. He separated out a portion of the dark gray into another pile and added a little white, lightening the dark gray a little. He continued to add white and make lighter and lighter piles of gray across the top of the pallet and finished with a pile of paint that was barely distinguishable from the white paint on the pallet.

He studied the old photograph of the Zeigfeld girl that he had taped to the top of his easel then studied his painting of the girl below it. He rested his hand on his maulstick and painted in a mid-gray strand of hair. He focused on line, shape, and value. He forgot he was sick. Everything but the painting faded away for a time.

"How's the painting going," Beth said, standing in the studio doorway, mail in one hand, lemonade in the other. She had bits of grass
and pine needles on her jeans and a smudge of dirt on her forehead.

Ben tore off a paper towel from the roll he always kept on the
floor when he painted. "Come and look," he said.

Beth stepped closer, and Ben wiped the smudge from her forehead.

"Oh," she said, "Any more?"

"No, just that."

She said thanks and leaned forward and kissed him. She narrowed her eyes and looked the painting up and down and then
studied the old photograph.

"I like it," she said, "but..."

"But?"

"Well...you're not using any color?"

"No, just gray scale. I may add some color. I don't know. I still
have a long way to go."

"Well, while you were in here painting your bleak picture, I got
some shots of the hummingbird at the feeder in the backyard."

"Nice. You'll have to show me."

"I don't know, you may not like them."

"Why?"

"They're full of color." Beth shot a glance at Ben's canvas.

"Oh right." Ben looked at the grayscale painting over his shoulder. "You know," he said, turning back to Beth, "I think I'm going to take down that hummingbird feeder and put up a bat house."

Beth shuffled off to the shower and Ben thumbed through the mail, bills, court notices, Rolling Stone and Vanity Fair and Hot Bike magazines, and a little hand addressed envelope, return address: "Jakob Snyder, Inmate #12745, Secure Psychiatric Unit, NH State prison...."

Ben tore the envelope and unfolded the letter. "Dear Attorney Truitt," it read, "Iłk'idą́, kǫǫ yá'édįná'a. I want to extend my gratitude to you for representing my love, my Gina, so well."

Ben sat on his painting stool. The letter continued: "I am thankful for you, sir. It is very important to me to keep Gina safe and out of jail..."

And it's important to me to keep her safe, out of jail, off the sex offender registry and away from you, Ben thought.

"... and you have done that for her. She is a fine woman and mother. She is the greatest gift I could have ever given my children."

OK.

"You see, much of my current predicament and my trouble with women, stems from my mother. My mother emotionally abandoned me when I was very young. I move from woman to woman because I fear they, too, will only abandon me in time. Deep down I fear I am not worthy of a woman's love. I fear I am not worthy of the love of a fine woman like Gina."

Ben turned the page.

"I am highly intelligent. I know when I'm being duped."

Ben turned back to the bottom of the first page to see if he had missed anything. He hadn't.

"I have had visions since I was very young. Many of the visions have come true, like the Oklahoma City bombing, David Koresh and Waco, Texas, tsunamis, earthquakes, hurricanes, Ronald Reagan, the return of Hong Kong to the Chinese. These were all signs and validations of my gift.

"The truth is I have been involved in a spiritual struggle for nearly one hundred years now. I am a full being. My mind is integrated. There is an evil that pervades this world, penetrates our institutions, and seeps into our minds if we are not vigilant. It is this spirit that decimated the Lakota and the Crow and the Apache. I am white and Apache and the chosen vehicle to dispatch this evil. You see, I am born of both worlds, the red and the white, and the struggle rages within me and without. I have read from the black bible and my eyes did not burn. I have plucked the eye of my most formidable foe and rendered him weaker in the next world.

"I have enclosed bath soaps in this envelope. They have aromatic healing powers. Keep them with you and breath them always."

Ben looked in the envelope. There was a little brown bar of soap in the corner. It smelled of lye.

The letter continued: "Sir, I couldn't help but overhear you in the courtroom on the 24th of February. Forgive me for eavesdropping. But I love Gina so and miss her. I needed to hear her voice and hear about her world without me. I couldn't help myself. I heard about your lovely wife, Beth."

"Shit," Ben whispered.

"And my heart soared to hear of her and the love you have for her. I wish her grand luck with her photography. As Gina said that day, art is a difficult path. But I believe in destiny and what is meant to be will be. The most important part is that you support her, and it sounds like you do."

Ben turned to page three. "Mr. Truitt, sir, I do not believe my current lawyer has my best interests at heart. He is not representing me to the best of his abilities."

Ben knew what was coming.

"Not the way you have represented my Gina."

"I'm getting hungry?" Beth called from the kitchen, "Are you?"

"Yes," Ben called back. "I was thinking of making some mushroom and cheese omelets."

"Sounds good."

 "Be there in a minute."

Ben continued reading: "He wants me to use some kind of insanity defense. Insanity...me? Eccentric maybe, but insane, I think not. I'm looking at 40-80 years in prison. I have so much to do. I have a prophecy to fulfill. I can't be in prison for 80 years."

Then maybe listen to your lawyer, Ben thought.

 Snyder then asked Ben to come to the prison and talk to him and maybe take his case or at least help him in any way that "he might be so kind." The letter ended with "Gotál jiis'áí 'áee, Mai tsíbąąee naaná'azhishná'a."

Even if I hadn't represented a key witness against you in a related case, Ben thought, I wouldn't touch your case. "Not with a ten-foot pole." he said, walking to the kitchen and stuffing the letter back into the envelope and the envelope into his pocket.

"Talking to yourself again?" Beth was standing at the sink looking out the window to the backyard.

"Yup," Ben said, coming up behind her. "The doctors tell me it's OK as long as I don't answer." He wrapped his hands around Beth's waist and kissed her neck.

"Mmmm," she said.

"Do you think I deserve you?" he asked.

"Not in a million years." She spun in his arms to face him, putting her arms around his neck. "Why do you ask?"

"No reason."

CHAPTER EIGHT
Monday, June 6, 2017

The apartments on the south end of Union Street in Manchester were stacked on asphalt lots like LEGO blocks, three stories high and colorless with corroded iron landings at each level. The doors to each apartment, five to a level, stood grey in the afternoon sun and even the curtains that hung in the small windows seemed depleted of any recognizable color. Eighteen years ago, apartment three on the first floor belonged to Eva and Emmanuel Guardia. Eighteen years ago, apartment twelve on the third floor belonged to Florence Laduc.

The iron rails of the narrow stairways scratched Ben's hands and the smell of dry rust filled his nose as he climbed the stairs to apartment twelve. After Eva's court hearing and their encounter with Jakob Snyder, Ben re-read the police reports in Eva's file.

For months after her arrest, Eva insisted that someone else had killed Manny. She called the El Paso Police Department and told the receptionist that Jakob Snyder had killed Manny. After several months

*of medication and talk therapy, she abandoned that idea and decided
that her thoughts and visions of Jakob Snyder in her apartment that
night were hallucinatory and delusional, her mind's attempt to pro-
tect her from the horror of the truth.*

Ben stepped up on the metal grate of the second-floor landing.

*Florence Ludac, however, told the Manchester Police that she had
seen a man leaving Eva's apartment the day Manny died.*

Ben ascended the narrow staircase to the third floor. Apartment
twelve was the second colorless door on his right. He knocked,
waited, knocked again. The venetian blind covered half the window, and inside the apartment looked dark. He pounded the door,
nothing. He turned back to the stairwell. He had walked down
five stairs when he smelled cigarette smoke and heard a congested
voice.

"Yeah?"

Florence Laduc looked about seventy-five. She was probably about
fifty-five. Natural Light cans and ashtrays littered her apartment.
The smell of stale cigarettes hung in the air. A nearly empty bottle
of bottom shelf bourbon stood on her kitchen counter, and a dry
bottle of Jose Cuervo laid on the floor.

"Would you like some coffee?" Flo asked, motioning Ben to
have a seat at her red and chrome kitchen table.

"No, thank you," Ben said and sat at the table. "I'm good." The
table and the chair felt sticky.

"What time is it, anyway?" she asked, wiping her forehead with the back of her hands.

"It's about one o'clock," Ben said.

"Oh, in that case," Flo said and opened her refrigerator. She pulled out a Natural Light tall can and cracked it open. "Coffee is like plasma to me, but sometimes I need whole blood." She took a gulp and sat down at the table across from Ben. "Who are you again?" Flo rubbed the heel of her palm into her eye.

Ben handed her a card. She read it. "Well, Benjamin Truitt, Esquire, what brings you here?"

"Eva Guardia, do you remember her?"

Flo's face went still. She shook a Kool cigarette from her pack, pulled off the filter, lit it, and took a long drag. "Of course, I remember Eva," She said with an exhale of smoke. "She's not someone you forget."

"I'd like to ask you some questions about her and about what happened here eighteen years ago, if that's all right."

Flo turned her eyes to the nearly empty bottle of bourbon on her kitchen counter. "Have you ever tried Knob Creek?"

Ben told her he had and promised to buy her a bottle when they were done talking.

"Eva and I were buds," Flo said. "We liked to drink and smoke cigarettes and weed together out on the landing on nice nights. In the winter, we took it inside." Flo pulled a bit of tobacco from the tip of her tongue. "I knew Eva had problems. So…" Flo paused and her eyes searched Ben's face.

"So?" Ben asked.

"So, do I," Flo said. "So, we self-medicated together."

"Oh," Ben said, looking up from his yellow pad. "What problems...if you don't mind my asking...what problems do you..."

"PTSD," Flo said. Her face was expressionless. "I was abused as a worker in the sex industry, among other things."

"Oh, I'm sorry." Ben had been Lyme disease free for several years, but as he studied Flo's face, he felt some of the old depression wash over him.

"Don't worry," Flo said and took a swig from the can. "I have medicine."

Ben nodded.

Flo took another swig. "Eva scared the shit out of some of the other tenants sometimes," Flo said.

"Really?"

"No shit-for-brains, I'm lying."

"OK," Ben said, "sorry."

"She scared the shit out of Joanie Cole. Eva used to stare at Joanie and ask Joanie if she was alive or dead. Joanie would freak and ask, 'What do you mean, Eva, what do you mean?' Eva would just stare."

"That didn't bother you?" Ben asked.

"No, Eva was tiny, and I never saw her do anything physical to anyone. She was more likely to withdraw into herself like one of her little pet turtles than to lash out, and she was so sweet with Manny."

"Really?"

Flo gave Ben the stink eye.

"Sorry," Ben said.

"Yes. She worshiped that kid. He was her world."

"Was she acting differently around the time Manny died?"

"Yeah." Flo walked over to the refrigerator and pulled out another tall can. "She wasn't coming around and drinking with me as much." Flo smiled. "So, I was worried that she wasn't medicating properly."

Ben nodded.

"I heard she was telling the neighbors about having dreams about being pulled down to hell and red people. She asked them if they thought Manny was a good boy. She was saying things like if the evil lived in her she should be destroyed. She asked me if my eyes burned when I read the black bible."

"What did you say to that?" Ben asked.

"I said, 'Have another beer, Eva.'" Flo crushed her cigarette out in the ashtray on the table. "Some of the neighbors told Eva she should see a doctor or counselor or someone."

"Do you know if she saw anyone?"

"I don't think so. She told me she was afraid the state would take Manny if she saw someone." Flo ripped the filter off another Kool. "Manny was all she had."

Ben flipped the page of his yellow pad. "Did you see a man leaving Eva's apartment the day Manny died?"

"Who told you that?"

"I read it in the police reports," Ben said.

Flo leaned back in her chair.

Ben chose his words carefully. "The reports said that you later said you were mistaken."

"Yeah."

"What happened there?"

"I was mistaken." Flo's voice was distant.

"Oh," Ben stood up. He clicked his pen and picked up his yellow pad. "Where's the nearest liquor store?"

"On Hanover Street," Flo said, "by the..."

"Aloha Restaurant." Ben smiled. "I know it well."

When Ben turned into the parking lot, Flo was standing on the third-floor landing, looking down at him. Ben killed the engine, pulled off his helmet and hung it on the handlebars. He produced a carton of shrimp lo mein from one saddlebag and a bottle of Knob Creek bourbon from the other.

"A lawyer who rides a Harley." Flo laughed, "You gotta love it."

"Yeah, you do," Ben called back, as he walked across the parking lot. At a distance, in the afternoon light where you couldn't see the wrinkles and emaciation, Flo looked quite beautiful. She must have been something back in the day.

"You didn't have to," Flo said, taking the carton of lo mein. "The bourbon was plenty."

"I wanted to."

Ben agreed to stay and have a drink.

Flo opened the bourbon and poured some into two red plastic

cups. She put the cups and paper plates and plastic forks on the table.

Ben took a seat. The chair and the tabletop were damp, but the stickiness was gone.

After her third cup and a little lo mein, Flo said, "Look, it was Eva's brother or half-brother, I guess he was."

"What?" Ben was still working on his first cup of bourbon and his second plate of lo mein.

"The guy I saw leaving Eva's apartment that night, it was Eva's brother."

"Jakob?"

"Something like that, I think, but he went by some weird name. He came up from Texas or New Mexico somewhere for a few days." Flo lifted her cup. "Eva was so excited to introduce me to him. She was in awe of him. She told me he was a spirit man and a prophet. But he scared the shit out of me." Flo took a sip of bourbon.

"Why didn't anyone else mention him to the police?"

"I don't know. They probably didn't see him. I don't think Eva introduced him to anyone else while he was here. He barely left Eva's apartment. Eva and Manny barely left the apartment while he was here." Flo swirled the bourbon around in the bottom of her cup then downed it in a gulp. "I saw Jakob outside a couple of times around two or three in the morning under the streetlight at the edge of the parking lot."

Flo got up and poured herself another cup of Knob Creek. She stood, arms folded, looking into her cup, shaking her head from side to side. "I miss Eva, you know," Flo said. "I went to see her once in the psychiatric unit at the prison, but she was in a strange place. I'm not sure she knew who I was."

The south end of Union Street overflowed with people and one and two story rectangular buildings, apartments, ethnic groceries stores, bodegas, and little eating joints. The summer air smelled of barbeque and exhaust. The road was narrow and littered with pot holes and loose asphalt. Ben spotted a dirty needle on a drain grate on the corner of Union and Cedar. Every now and then, he stood on his foot pegs when the bike bounced over a bump or into a hole that he couldn't swerve around. On both sides of the road, adults of various ages and colors sat on staircases and smoked and listened to music, while children played jump rope on the sidewalks and rode bicycles in the street.

As Ben continued down Union Street, the road grew smoother and wider, eating joints disappeared, buildings spread farther apart, single-family homes replaced apartments. Oak trees lined both sides of the street and spread canopies overhead. Cars rested under carports or in garages. No one walked the sidewalks. The air smelled of flowers and Concord grapes. Ben saw no dirty needles. At the north end of Union Street, people altered consciousness behind locked doors.

CHAPTER NINE
Friday, June 10, 2017

"Where are you going today, Ben?" the receptionist's voice chirped through the metal speaker.

Ben peered through the glass at the receptionist and pressed the speak button on the intercom. "C Unit."

"And who are you going to see?" the speaker chirped again.

Ben rapped the glass with his knuckles. "Is this bulletproof?"

The receptionist's blue eyes flashed up at him. "That's what they tell us." She smiled, white teeth in a dark booth. "And who were you going to see again?"

"Jakob Snyder."

The receptionist dialed her phone and spoke, her voice muffled behind the glass. "Attorney Ben Truitt to see Jakob Snyder." She hung up the phone and wrote "C" on a blue and white sticker. "You're all set," she said and slid the sticker to Ben through the little trough under the glass.

"Thanks." Ben placed the sticker above the breast pocket of his suit.

"And Ben," the speaker said, "Jakob Snyder is a level 1."

"Ok."

A buzzer sounded, and the electronic door clicked open. Ben walked through the tall plants in the garden room on his way to C unit. A patient with a jagged gray beard sat in a Papa San chair bathing in the sunlight behind some potted palm trees.

He stopped in front of the C Unit door and pressed the call button. It buzzed inside. He peered through the reinforced glass opening in the thick wooden door. A mental health worker appeared from behind the wall at the end of the hallway. A couple of patients were playing checkers at the tables to the left of the door. One patient with a knit floppy hat and a goatee advanced to the door, peered through the glass at Ben, pivoted and strode away.

The mental health worker arrived at the door. He waved his keycard over the electronic sensor then took a key and unlocked the door handle. "Sorry," he said through the window, "it's a two-step process."

Ben stepped into the interview room and waited. He pulled a manila folder from his briefcase that contained a sweet-smelling, lumpy envelope. The envelope had arrived the day before and contained two bath soaps and a letter signed Gotal with a postscript that read, "Breath these always." It was the second letter Ben had received from Snyder in nine years.

The worker returned with Snyder. "He's a level one, so I have to stay with him."

"Can you wait outside the door?" Ben asked. "I'll be all right."

"Are you sure?"

"Yes," Ben said. "If there is another person in the room, we'll lose attorney-client confidentiality."

Snyder extended his hand. Ben shook it.

"I'll be right outside the door," the worker said.

Snyder took the seat across from Ben. "You got my letter."

"Yes."

"First," Snyder said, "I want to thank you for the wonderful work you did for Gina and Eva."

"There's no need for that."

"But I want to," Snyder said. "They are very important to me and you looked out for them." Snyder's voice was warm. He looked directly into Ben's eyes without blinking.

Ben tried to hold Snyder's gaze but kept turning his eyes to Snyder's face tattoo. "So, about your letter," Ben said.

"Will you represent me?"

"Well, let's talk about that."

Snyder told Ben that the superior court had found him incompetent to stand trial for the incest charges. A few weeks ago, he was transferred to New Hampshire Hospital. Ten days ago, the probate court committed him to five years at the hospital. "I can't stay here for five years," Snyder said, "I have too much to do."

"You don't necessarily have to stay here for five years," Ben explained. "When and if your doctors believe you're safe, they can release you on a conditional discharge."

"I know that," Snyder said, his voice cooling.

Ben studied Snyder's face tattoo, which from a distance looked like a random tribal design but up close seemed to be an animal form. A jagged and spiney ink line ran from the tip of Snyder's chin through the middle of his nose to his hairline, forming the edges of a tail and the back and head of some canine creature. The hind legs stretched across his face in hooks and sharp edges to his jawbone and the upper legs extended like scythe blades across the bridge of his nose to his temple. The animal's oversized genitalia were shaped like licks of flame and rolled down the side of his nose to his cheekbone. *Then again*, Ben thought, *maybe it's just an abstract design.*

"Well?" Snyder asked, when Ben stopped searching the tattoo.

"It's like a Rorschach test."

"It's a coyote, a powerful animal and an excellent tracker."

A predator and a trickster, Ben thought. "Did you do it yourself?"

"Yeah. What do you think?"

"He's well endowed."

"A symbol of great fertility."

"Well, I'm not much for tattoos." Ben had five hidden under his suit. His favorite was his first, Betty Boop in a little red dress. It reminded him of Beth.

The worker pressed his face closer to the door window. Ben

caught his eyes and gave him a little smile. The worker nodded and took a step back.

"They're giving me anti-psychotic drugs."

"What diagnosis have they given you?" Ben asked.

"Schizoaffective disorder, bipolar type," Snyder said. "I'm not crazy." Snyder's voice rose and he bounced his legs rapidly.

The mental health worker pressed his face to the door window again. Ben smiled again. The worker tilted his head and continued to watch through the window.

"I have visions. I receive prophecies. My mind is one. Their minds are splintered."

"OK," Ben said.

"Why didn't you respond when I asked you for help eight years ago?"

"I couldn't represent you. Gina was a co-defendant in that case and a witness against you."

"Why have you come this time?"

"Because I have no conflict of interest in this case." That was true. "And I wanted to see if I could help you." That was a lie.

Snyder stilled himself and asked, "How is your wife?"

"My wife?"

"Yes, when I saw you in court that day with Gina. I heard you talk about your wife. You seemed so loving in the way you talked about her and your children. It filled my heart with pain for the damage I had done my family."

"My wife is fine."

"Does she still take the train from Exeter to Cambridge every morning?"

Ben didn't answer. He watched the coyote genitalia spilling down the side of Snyder's face.

"And your kids, how are they? How's your son's music going and your daughter's theater? They must be young adults by now."

Ben fought an urge to crush Snyder's throat. "You know what," he said, "I have got to get to another meeting shortly." He was free for the rest of the day. "We should talk about your situation."

"All right."

"The best thing you can do is be cool. Don't cause any disturbances here. Don't make anybody uneasy. Take the medications they want you to take."

"But I'm not crazy." Snyder said. "The drugs make me feel synthetic, divided, partial. I'm not me on those drugs. I lose my visions. I become like them, like you, blunted and half alive."

"Look," Ben said, "even though it may not feel like it, you are the only one who can control your situation here. All the doctors can do is watch you and make recommendations for your treatment."

"Well…"

"You are in control. If you go along with them and do what they ask you to do and be cool, they will release you. If you refuse medications, if you tell them that you disagree with their diagnosis of you, they will keep you here. OK?"

"OK."

"You're a smart guy," Ben said. "You know what to do?"

"Yes."

Both men were quiet for a bit. Ben stuffed the manila folder and yellow pad back into his briefcase.

"Say hello to Gina and Eva for me will you," Snyder said, beginning to stand.

"I haven't seen Gina in years, but," Ben said, "about Eva…"

"Yeah?"

"In the police reports, someone said that you had been visiting her around the time that Manny died."

"Someone said, huh?"

"Yeah, I mean, I asked Eva about it, but she either didn't remember or she has buried all of that so deep…you know?"

"I know."

"Were you visiting her around that time?"

Snyder narrowed his eyes and turned and knocked on the door and the mental health worker opened it. He turned back to Ben and stared. His stare was ice. "You can't believe everything you hear," he said. "You should know that. Thank you for all your help, Attorney Truitt. I think you have given me good advice."

Ben grabbed a mental health worker who was walking by as he stepped out of the interview room. "Could you let me out?"

"Sure," she said, smiling. "You don't want to stay?"

"No."

"No one ever wants to stay." The worker unlocked the electronic lock with a keycard, unlocked the physical lock with a brass key, and let Ben out.

CHAPTER TEN

October 4, 2017

Ben opened the flaps to his saddlebags and dropped in the bags of groceries: shrimp, butter, Tabasco, scallions, garlic, and angel hair pasta. It was about 5:45 in the evening. The air smelled cool and clean. His pocket vibrated, and he pulled out his phone. It was Beth.

"Hey, babe," Ben said.

"Where have you been?" Beth's voice sounded broken.

"What's going on? Are you all right?"

"I've been calling and calling. Someone slashed my tires."

"What? Where are you?"

"I'm at the train station. The police have already been here. I called a tow truck."

"But you're all right."

"My fucking tires are slashed, Ben."

"OK. I'm on my way." Ben looked down at his phone. Seven missed calls from Beth, 5:10, 5:12, 5:17, 5:25, 5:26, 5:37, and 5:40 PM.

He dropped the loaf of Italian bread on the pavement and started the bike. He dropped the bike into first gear and rode about ten feet before circling back to the bread. Beth would be disappointed if there was no Italian bread with the shrimp scampi.

Ben laid on the throttle all the way to Exeter. He roared into the train station parking lot and saw a tow truck. The driver said he found the car but there was no one with it.

"No petite, dark haired woman?"

"No one," the driver said and ran the back of his hand across his nose and sniffed.

Ben gave the driver directions to his home and shot off to the Exeter police station.

The police officer had been to the train station. He spoke to Beth. She was upset, but all right. He investigated the scene, no witnesses at the station, no witnesses in neighboring businesses, no cameras in the area. "Don't worry," the officer said. "She probably got a ride home with a friend."

Ben called and called Beth's phone from the police station parking lot. The phone rang and rang. After the eighth or ninth time, the calls went directly to voicemail.

Ben found Beth's Toyota safely deposited in the driveway when he got home. He pulled his bike in behind the Toyota, tore off his gloves and helmet and threw them on the lawn. The house doors were locked. The lights were off. Ben called Beth's friends from the train. Some answered. Beth was upset about the tires, but fine, they said.

Ben paced from room to room. No keys hung on the peg in the kitchen, no coat in the hall closet, no shoes in the bedroom. His phone buzzed in his pocket. The caller ID read Tom Bartleby, Ben's accountant. He let it go to voicemail then listened. His taxes were ready to sign. When was he available?

Ben looked at his phone history again: seven missed calls from Beth, one connection; nine unanswered calls to Beth; three calls to Beth's friends; two missed calls from Gina Cataldo, 6:10, and 6:17 PM. Gina Cataldo? Ben hit call back.

Gina answered. "Hello."

"Hi, Gina. It's Ben Truitt. Remember me?"

"Yes, of course. How have you been?"

Ben looked at Beth's car through the kitchen window and rattled the keys in his hand. "Look," he said, "I'm calling because I saw you called me a couple times."

"I did? Odd," Gina said, "I must have dialed you accidentally." Gina laughed. "You know, butt dialed."

"Yeah, yeah, ok."

"Are you all right?" Gina asked.

Ben turned from the kitchen window and paced down the hallway to the living room. "I'm fine."

"You sound a little frazzled."

"I'm fine, really," Ben said. "It's just my wife is a little late coming home from work, and I'm worried, that's all."

"I'm sure she's fine," Gina said after a moment. "She'll be home any minute. You'll see."

Ben stopped rattling his keys and studied one of Beth's photographs on the living room wall, a red cardinal against a backdrop of snow covered birch trees. "Well, maybe you're right," he said. "Sorry to bother you." He pulled the phone from his ear and started to hang up.

"So how have you been otherwise?" Gina asked. "It's been years."

Ben put the phone back to his ear. "I can't complain, otherwise," he said. "You?"

"Good, good. I moved to the Maine coast. I live and fish with cousin Billie, now."

"Did you sell the place in New Canaan?"

"I tried. No takers. I guess it was too isolated."

"So, the place is just abandoned?"

"As far as I know," Gina said. "I haven't been there in years."

Ben heard a thud. "What was that?"

"Just one of the kids," Gina said. "He's still a bit wild. Must get it from his father."

Ben and Gina were silent. Ben stepped toward another one of Beth's photos and studied it, a boy and a girl with flowers painted on their faces laughing at a Portsmouth street fair.

"I saw him about a month ago, you know?" Ben said after a time.

"Jakob?"

"Yeah, he wrote me, so I went to see him at the hospital."

"I heard he was out," Gina said.

"What?" Ben heard more bumping noises.

"Or maybe not. Look, Ben, sorry. I got to go and get this kid under control." Gina hung up.

Jakob Snyder's voice played in Ben's mind. "How is your wife?" Ben shook his head. "When I saw you in court that day with Gina. I heard you talk about your wife. You seemed so loving in the way you talked about her and your children."

Ben dialed Tony Shevchenko. He saw Snyder's smile, heard Snyder's voice, "Does she still take the train from Exeter to Cambridge every morning?"

"Ben, Ben," Shev said, "seven forty-five on a week night. I'm off duty."

"Tony, did you know that the hospital released Jakob Snyder?"

"Yes, of course, about a week ago. We're on top of it. The New Canaan Police are keeping a close eye..."

"He's back in New Canaan?"

"Yeah, yeah. Are you all right? He moved back in with Gina."

Ben stopped breathing.

"Ben?" Shev paused. "Ben," he said, "nothing we could do. He was found incompetent, never convicted of anything. She dropped the restraining order. Nothing we could do. Ben?"

"I got to go." Ben said.

"What's going on? What's wrong?"

Ben hung up. He ran downstairs to his basement gun safe and

unlocked it. He grabbed his .45 and two loaded magazines from the safe and stuffed them into the gun pocket of his motorcycle jacket.

CHAPTER ELEVEN

Tripping

Ben took the bike as far as he could down Goodman Young Way, New Canaan, until it became impassible. He ran the remaining three hundred yards or so to Gina Cataldo's house.

The house emerged tall and dark on a hill against the night sky, barely lit by the half-moon. Ben climbed the steps of the farmer's porch and knocked on the door. The knock echoed hollow within. He walked along the side of the house, peeking through the black windows as he made his way around. Every now and then, a shard of moonlight lit shapes within the house, but nothing discernible, maybe a desk, maybe a rifle leaning against a wall, maybe a dream catcher hanging in a doorway. He couldn't be sure. He saw no shapes of people, no movement.

An orange glow crowned the night sky in the distance behind the house. Ben followed a path in the woods at the edge of the backyard that seemed to lead in that direction. The path was heavily overgrown and disappeared and reappeared before him in the half-light of the moon. The path wound and meandered but moved him toward the orange sky. A sharp scrub pine scratched the side his face. Crickets chirped. Something rustled in the bushes as Ben pressed on toward the light above and ahead of him. Here and there, he caught whiffs of burning firewood.

Ben felt something cold, and his body went rigid.

"Easy."

Ben looked to his left without moving his head. A gun muzzle rested on his shoulder and pressed against his neck.

"Jakob?" Ben asked.

"It's all right. Beth is there," Snyder said motioning with the gun barrel toward the orange sky. "She's good. In fact, she's better."

"What…?"

"Shhh," Jakob said and eased the gun barrel off Ben's neck. "Turn around slowly."

Ben turned and saw Snyder, half in the path and half in the trees. He was bare-chested, wearing nothing but an animal skin vest and jeans. He pulled a flask from his back pocket, unscrewed the cap, and extended it to Ben. "I need you to drink this," he said.

"What is it?" Ben asked.

"Drink it!" Snyder snapped.

Ben took the flask and sniffed it.

"Drink it," Snyder said softly and pressed the gun into the center of Ben's forehead.

Ben took a mouthful.

"Swallow." Snyder poked Ben's forehead twice with the gun.

Ben swallowed what tasted like apple wine.

"One more."

Ben took another mouthful and swallowed.

"Good," Snyder said and held out his hand.

Ben handed the flask back to Snyder, who stepped fully into the path.

"Now, turn and walk." Snyder motioned down the path with the rifle.

Ben turned. "Jakob," he said.

"In silence," Snyder said, "in silence. You will see." He laughed. "In silence, you will see." Snyder jabbed Ben in the back, and Ben began to walk.

"Gotal," Synder said, "Gotal now and forever." Snyder fell silent for a time, and the two men snaked their way through the woods.

"The path gets obscured ahead," Snyder said, "and I wanted to guide you the right way. Soon, you'll see. You'll understand." Snyder spoke rapidly, but softly. "There is a barrier between the conscious and unconscious minds. Most live half lies...see through glass darkly ...believe half-truths. But some live fully...Jesus, yes... Geronimo, yes...all true spirit men, really. Do you know today they would be labeled mentally ill? Today, they would be given antipsychotic medications. Today, they would be pharmaceutically incarcerated. They don't need Thorazine. They don't need Haldol. No, no, not drugs to block the pathways between their conscious and unconscious minds, not drugs to castrate them and silence the many voices of god..."

The path disappeared before Ben and he stopped short. He felt the gun jab into his spine.

"This is the spot," Snyder said. "Just push through that thicket." He prodded Ben with the barrel.

Ben shouldered through a wall of sharp scrub pines, and everything disappeared into black. "No." Ben heard Snyder's voice softly behind him. "No, the doctors...no, the people need hallucinogens to restore the pathways of their minds. Your pathways are blocked. Mine are clear. It's not mental illness. It's enlightenment, you see. You will see, Ben Truitt."

Ben continued to shoulder and weave through the dense woods. Sharp branches and pine needles scratched his hands and cheeks. He raised his hands and pushed through a large branch that hung about chin high, the needles sticky and sweet. He let the branch go as he passed and heard it whip back behind him as he stepped into a small clearing alone.

Two pathways appeared at the end of the clearing, one running toward the orange glow in the night sky, and the other running into blackness, or at least into nothing that Ben could discern.

He started down the path toward the orange light, which at times seemed to turn crystal green and emit a sound like a singing bowl. Slants of moonlight filtered through the trees ahead of him and cascaded down the path like river rapids. He stepped into rushing white water, amazed to find only a puddle of light.

He continued down the path as it rose and fell and twisted. He took long strides to keep from falling off, and he jutted his arms out from time to time for balance. The darkness was palpable with a thick taste like honey. *Fight this*, he thought. He pushed his long hair back with both hands. His forehead was wet with sweat, and his ears pounded.

The path spilled down a hill and opened into a clearing below. In the center of the clearing, the moon lodge pulsated yellow and orange and green. Blue smoke whispered through a large hole in the center of the roof.

CHAPTER TWELVE

The Moon Lodge

The moon lodge was shaped like a mushroom top made of bent tree boughs and animal skins. Light from within throbbed red against the skins and exposed shadows and silhouettes against the walls. The lodge looked like a living organism to Ben. He pictured it scuttling away through the forest like some giant firebug.

Ben stepped quietly to the side of the lodge and peered in through a round opening cut into the skin wall. A primal drumbeat filled the room. Ben saw Snyder dancing close to the fire. He was naked except for a red cloth that draped his genitals. His torso and thighs glistened with sweat and blue and white paint. He chanted something in a low monotone as Gina Cataldo swayed next to him in time to the same beat. Her hair spilled down her back and a large feather dangled to one side. She tilted her head toward the opening in the center of the roof and closed her eyes. She was barefooted and dressed only in a suede bikini top and an animal skin loincloth. Her belly and thighs were painted blue and white. Her entire body shined with sweat and looked greasy in the fire light.

The center of the lodge blazed high and low as the bonfire rose and fell. The edges of the lodge lit red as the fire roared and then fell back into shadow as the flames retreated. Ben saw no drum or drummer. Shadow people came through the walls.

Snyder stopped his chanting and commanded, "Come here now, Beth."

Beth stepped out of a shadow edge and into the flaming center of the lodge. Two shadow women walked with her. Beth's hair was tossed all over her head. Her mascara dribbled down her cheeks, and purple bruises blossomed her face. She was clothed like Gina. Her torso was painted in pink and white tribal designs, and her bare legs were either bleeding or painted red. She trembled as she moved to Snyder's side.

Rage welled in Ben's chest. The .45 rested cold and heavy in his jacket against his ribs. He fidgeted with the cell phone in his pants pocket.

Snyder pointed to a spot on the ground in front of him and Beth stepped to it, her back to Ben. Ben spotted hand-shaped bruises on Beth's upper arms and on the back and inside of her thighs.

Snyder stared directly at Ben. "Please," Snyder said pointing at a spot on the ground next to Beth.

Ben moved away from the window. The ground moved under him and rolled him through the door of the lodge to the spot where Snyder pointed. A wind followed behind Ben and blew the shadow women to shards.

"This is a day of liberation for you both." Snyder smiled and raised his hands, palms uplifted. "You will understand the true nature of your mind when the shroud between your conscious and unconscious mind is torn, when the barrier between male and female is broken, when your spirit and your sex are one." Snyder flashed his eyes over Beth. He lowered one hand and ran it over his loincloth, keeping the other hand uplifted. His face dripped molten liquid in the firelight as his hand slid over his genitals.

Gina swayed and rolled her hips at Snyder's side.

The drum throbbed on.

Ben stood like a stone. Rage welled in his chest. Flames rose behind him and reflected green and red in Snyder's eyes.

Gina turned her gaze to the opening in the ceiling and began to grow toward the night sky beyond.

"You see, Jesus knew these things," Snyder said. "It's all there... Geronimo knew these things and Isaiah...and the centurions who were one in one hundred. You will know." Snyder's eyes moved from Beth to Ben and back. The fire quieted behind them and soft white light fell on Snyder's face. He looked kind to Ben in this light, transfigured in soft yellows, and the silence weighed heavy against Ben's body.

Gina rolled her hips to the primal drum as she stretched closer to the sky. Flames followed her through the hole in the ceiling, licked at the edges, and plunged deeply into the dark opening.

Beth took Ben's hand gently. He felt it cold and trembling.

"But first, Ben," Snyder said, rubbing the palms of his hands all over his bald pate, "your little mystery...I know why you came to see me at the hospital. Do you think I'm stupid? I told you I wasn't. You didn't believe me? Do you need proof?" Snyder's voice grew with every question, and his words hung in the air around him.

Gina stopped swaying and folded back into her body.

The drumbeat stopped. Beth convulsed in a sob and began to fall slowly into the earth beneath her feet.

"Here's the thing," Snyder whispered. "Yes," he shouted. "The answer is yes. Yes, I did, but that child was the spawn of evil. It was in the prophecy that my sister and I received as children. Eva and I were two together. We chased visions together. We melted into the desert. We learned of a powerful child, a shape-shifter, a demon. I traveled east following the prophecy, as it was written. It was true. It is true. The true nature of the child was revealed to me in a flash, in an instant. The knife appeared before me. The boy read from the black bible. Eva wasn't there, not in the room. It was done as it had to be done, quickly, dispassionately. You see? I took the eye to weaken the demon in the next world."

Ben saw a flash and heard a crack that split the air and rang in his ears. Snyder's head snapped back. Red paint spread along his forehead and flowed down his face. Snyder's legs buckled, and he collapsed to the ground.

White noise buzzed in Ben's ears. Beth squeezed his side. He saw her crying but heard nothing.

A silent movie unfolded before Ben. Tony Shevchenko appeared in the lodge entrance, looked around and holstered his gun. He grabbed Gina by the shoulders. His mouth moved. Gina nodded, backed into the shadows, and squatted.

Shev turned to Ben and Beth. His mouth moved. Ben heard white noise. Shev shook his head, moved his mouth. White noise. He pointed to the body. White noise.

Shev found Snyder's .30/.30 leaning against a wall. He cocked and fired the rifle, cocked and fired, cocked and fired. Two shots smashed into a tree bow above the window and the third sliced through the skin wall to the right of the window opening.

Shev pulled a handkerchief from his pocket and wiped down the rifle. He bent over Snyder and unfolded Snyder's right hand, carefully placing the rifle grip in the hand and placing the index finger on the trigger. He turned to Gina, who cowered in the shadows. Shev wagged his finger and flapped his jaws at Gina, who did not look up.

Shev walked over to Ben and Beth. He took his coat off and wrapped it around Beth's shoulders. He stood in front of the two and looked from one to the other and shook his head.

Ben caught bits of Shev's words through the white noise. He thought he heard "Jesus" and "tripping." Ben looked down at Snyder. He saw that half of Snyder's face was gone, only the tribal tattoo remained, writhing in the firelight.

"You know what happened, right?" Ben heard Shev hollering from, what sounded like, a great distance away.

Ben nodded. He yelled, "Yes," but only heard it inside his head.

CHAPTER THIRTEEN

Full Circle

The newspapers reported that Police Captain Tony Shevchenko shot and killed Jakob Snyder in New Canaan, NH, after Snyder opened fire on Shevchenko as Shevchenko was attempting to arrest Snyder for kidnapping. The reports stated that Snyder kidnapped his former girlfriend, Gina Cataldo, Benjamin Truitt, a lawyer, and Truitt's wife, M.I.T. lecturer and freelance photographer, Elizabeth Truitt. Snyder, who referred to himself as Gotal, suffered from schizophrenia and believed himself to be the reincarnation of an Apache medicine man. His only known relative was a half-sister who lived in the Concord area and did not wish to be identified.

Ben knocked on Eva's door. Eva opened the door the width of the chain lock and stuck her face in the opening. "Attorney Truitt," she said, "I got your message. Is everything OK with my case? They are not going to send me back to SPU, are they?"

"No, no," Ben said. "Everything is all right, really."

Eva's eyes narrowed. "Well, why..."

"I'll explain," Ben said. "Could I come in?"

Eva looked Ben up and down and unlatched the door. She opened it wide enough to let Ben edge through.

"I brought someone with me," Ben said.

Florence Laduc stepped into the doorway, "Hey bud," she said and opened her arms for a hug. "I've missed you."

Eva took a step back.

Flo dropped her arms to her sides. "I can go," she said.

Eva took Flo by the hand. "No," she said. "Come in, please. I'm sorry."

The three sat around a coffee table in Eva's little living area. The air in the room smelled of pine air fresheners.

"Nice place," Flo said.

"Thanks," Eva said. "So, what's going on?"

Ben pulled a cell phone from his pocket. "Well," he said, "there's something I want you to hear." He placed the phone on the coffee table and turned the volume to full. "It's a little muffled so you may have to lean in."

Eva leaned in.

Ben pressed play: "But first, Ben, your little mystery..."

"Is that Jakob?" Eva asked

"Yes," Ben said, pausing the recording.

"It's hard to hear."

"I know," Ben said, "but listen..."

"I know why you came to see me at the hospital. Do you think I'm stupid? I told you I wasn't. You didn't believe me? Do you need proof?"

"Is someone crying?" Eva asked.

"Yes," Ben said, "listen..."

"Here's the thing...The answer is yes. Yes, I did, but that child was the spawn of evil. It was in the prophecy that my sister and I received as children. Eva and I were two together. We chased visions together. We melted into the desert. We learned of a powerful child, a shape-shifter, a demon. I traveled east following the prophecy, as it was written. It was true. It is true. The true nature of the child was revealed to me in a flash, in an instant. The knife appeared before me. The boy read from the black bible. Eva wasn't there, not in the room. It was done as it had to be done, quickly, dispassionately. You see?"

Ben stopped the recording.

Eva leaned back in her chair, and something happened. Maybe it was the way light and shadow fell in the room, maybe it was Ben's imagination, maybe it was a flashback from whatever hallucinogens Snyder had slipped him in the apple wine, but a shell fell from Eva and light and warmth rose from her and filled the room. Eva smiled and sobbed, her face wet and shining.

Flo pulled a bottle of Patron from her handbag. Eva disappeared into the kitchen and returned with three shot glasses on a tray with a pile of salt and lime wedges.

Flo filled the glasses, raised hers, and said, "To self-medication."

"To self-medication," Eva said, raising her glass.

Ben shook his head, clinked his glass with theirs, shot his tequila, and bit a lime slice.

After the third round, they all ate sugar skulls and proclaimed no fear of death. After the fifth round, Eva produced an old photograph of Jakob from an end table drawer and passed it around to Ben and Flo. The shot was candid, Jakob alone in a desert landscape, caught in mid-laugh. He looked about sixteen, clean and innocent. Long blond hair draped across his forehead and down his shoulders. His eyes beamed.

Eva took the photo from Ben and walked it over to the Ofrenda and placed Jakob's image on the table before the Santa Muerta figure. She returned to the others and sat down. "He was my blood," she said.

CHAPTER FOURTEEN

Two or more witnesses

The Hanover Street Chop House sat on the corner of Pine and Hanover street, a posh oasis in a blue-collar city. Outside, the Chop House fronted stonewalls, brass rails, and red awnings. Inside, soft light complimented the middle-aged clientele, and mahogany wainscoting ran from floor to ceiling. The waitstaff wore white tops and black bottoms and addressed the steak eaters and scotch and wine drinkers as sir or ma'am. Tony Shevchenko stored his best bottles of wine in the Chop House cellar, and when he dined he told the staff which bottles to open for the night.

"A shell fell from her body?" Shev thumbed his glass of scotch and shot a glance across the table at Beth. "And warmth filled the room?"

"I'm telling you," Ben said, "you could feel it."

"You were still tripping," Shev said. "He was still tripping. Right, Beth?"

"I don't know," Beth said. "It could be."

"Artists," Shev said in mock disgust, "romantics. You see, you need guys like me to keep the bad man from the door, so you can have your liberal attitudes."

"Here we go," Ben said.

"What?" Shev asked as the waiter arrived at the table. "I'll have the Brandt Farms 16-ounce ribeye, medium, baked potato, asparagus with hollandaise sauce," Shev said before the waiter could hand out the menus.

"Same," Ben said.

"Same," Beth said, "but medium-rare."

"Very good." The waiter slipped the menus back into his apron.

"You don't come to the Chop House for rabbit food," Shev said.

"No, you don't," Beth agreed.

"And two more Scotches, please," Ben said.

"Very good," the waiter said and disappeared into the kitchen.

"How's Gina doing?" Ben asked Shev.

"She's OK, but she has got to be the most passive woman I have ever met."

"Poor thing," Beth said running her index finger along the edge of her wine glass.

"She's onboard with what happened?"

"Yup, she understands that it all happened just like the newspapers and the police reports described," Shev said. "She was tripping so hard, though, I'm not sure she knows one way or the other."

The waiter returned with a fresh round of drinks, placed them on red napkins in front of the three, and cleared the empty glasses.

"And if she starts to get lucid about that night," Shev said, after the waiter faded back into the kitchen, "I pulled enough weed and peyote and LSD from her house to remind her to forget."

Ben took a sip of his Johnnie Walker Black, and Beth circled her finger around the rim of her wine glass.

Shev studied their faces. "He murdered a little boy," he said.

"He did," Ben said.

Beth nodded, her eyes tracking her circling finger.

"He kidnapped Beth." Shev raised his glass. "Come on," he said, "to consistent stories."

Ben studied the crowd in the dining room.

"C'mon."

Ben rattled the ice in his glass then raised it to Shev's. "Consistent stories," he said.

Beth stopped circling her finger and lifted her glass. "Consistent stories," she repeated.

Heavy rain fell, and the air blew cold as Ben and Beth stepped out of the restaurant. The valet eased Ben's Toyota to the entrance. He accepted a ten-dollar bill from Ben and shielded Beth with an umbrella as she walked to the passenger side door.

Ben made a right turn out of the parking lot onto Hanover Street and followed Hanover Street to Route 101 East. He took it slow on the highway, squinting through the rain and the glare from oncoming headlights. Beth sat quietly in the dark beside him, chewing on her bottom lip.

Ben thought about taking a long motorcycle ride in the morning, maybe to Route 1A along the seacoast to Little Boar's Head and Rye Beach and into Maine, or maybe north to the lakes, or maybe west through Dublin and Jaffrey to Mount Monadnock. He could grab a special sub at Moe's in Raymond and eat it under a pine tree and maybe read Thoreau or do some sketching.

"I think I might take a ride tomorrow."

"It's going to be cold," Beth said and returned to chewing her lip. Every now and then, she let out a long, slow exhale.

The windshield wipers clacked on the window. Ben turned up the heat, trying to chase away the cold and damp. He pushed a Chet Baker CD into the stereo.

After about eight miles passed, Beth said, "I fought him, you know."

"I know," Ben said softly.

"I wrestled Gina's phone from her and tried to call you."

Headlights from a westbound car flashed across Beth's face like a searchlight, and Ben saw tears in her eyes.

"We're screwed, right?" Beth asked.

Ben looked over at her and then back to the slick pavement ahead. "Well," he said.

"I mean covering up a murder." Beth stared at the side of Ben's face. "That's got to be..."

"Obstruction of justice, making a false report to a police officer, accomplice liability."

"Shit, Ben, why do you do this?"

Ben turned to look at Beth again but said nothing. He knew that, for a time anyway, he could bury all this in the same place he buried all the truths that his criminal clients had confided in him over the years. Beth had no such place.

Beth let out another long exhale. "And now you've pulled me into it."

Ben had no response. He took Exit 6 off Route 101 onto Beede Hill Road toward Epping. No streetlights lit the road and few cars traveled it at night. Roads just like Beede Hill Road wound all through the New Hampshire landscape. For twenty-eight years, Ben and Beth had traveled those roads together, side by side. Sometimes Ben drove, sometimes Beth. Tonight, with no moon and Ben driving, the road was particularly dark. Ben could only see to the end of the headlights, but that was enough to get them home.

www.ingramcontent.com/pod-product-compliance
Lightning Source LLC
Chambersburg PA
CBHW020327130626
46549CB00003B/1050